# THE PSYCHIC ON THE JURY

BRIAN C. E. BUHL

Published by Water Dragon Publishing
*waterdragonpublishing.com*

ISBN 978-1-962538-76-3 (Trade Paperback)

FIRST EDITION

10 9 8 7 6 5 4 3 2 1

*For Bryanna*

# THE PSYCHIC ON THE JURY

MY NAME IS MEL WALKER and, as a psychic, I spend most of my time chasing ghosts. I've run into a couple of people that tried to say I was a medium. I'm not so sure about that. Actual mediums summon spirits and allow them to enter their body and speak using their voice. As far as I know, I've never been possessed. I see ghosts, talk to them, and sometimes look into the past to help them find closure.

It's not much of a living. I get a stipend from The Society of Supernatural Investigations, which is just enough to keep me above the poverty line. I'm a little bit better off than when I worked as a repo man, but that's a different story.

I'm not complaining, but there are some drawbacks to this new lifestyle. When I used to live on the edge of someone's property, stealing electricity and having to take a shovel every time I needed to number two, I was somewhat invisible as far as the government was concerned. Things are different, now. I pay taxes four times a year. I'm on the grid, with hot and cold running water, and just enough extra money to eat pizza once a week instead of ramen. Also, I can now be summoned to sit on a jury.

I received my first summons after one of those mythical pizza nights. I got up just before the crack of noon — dealing with ghosts puts a person on the night shift, most of the time — and I picked up the mail after dropping the flattened boxes in the dumpster. I stood in front of the mailbox looking at a very official-looking document, thinking I might be in some kind of trouble. Across two different states, no good thing has ever come my way after getting entangled in the legal system. And this piece of paper said Sacramento County Courthouse on it.

A jury summons. They wanted me, of all people, to be on a jury. They had no idea what they were asking.

I read the finer details of the summons as I made my way back to my trailer. If I was reading it correctly, I might not have to go to the courthouse at all. I needed to call in at a certain time and if they didn't need me, I would be free. Even if they called me in, it was either going to be for one day, or one trial. This didn't have to be a big deal.

The thought of serving on a jury sat heavy on my mind as I cleaned up, got dressed, and made my way downtown to The Society's office. I daydreamed of sitting in a courtroom as two power attorneys battled it out in front of me, like gladiators in an arena. Only the unmistakable smell of human feces on the light rail broke me out of my fantasy, but I was right back to it after I shifted seats to one near an open window.

At The Society's office at 20th and K, I bypassed the conference room and ducked into the kitchen at the back of the building. "Kitchen" certainly described one of the functions of the room, as it had a gas oven, a microwave oven, industrial-looking sinks — plural — and a pair of refrigerators, one for human food and one for other weird things. Pedro Ortega and Bobby Greenwood sat across from each other at the small table near the back door, steaming cups of coffee in front of both men. I snagged the last sprinkled donut from a box on the counter before joining them.

"Breakfast of champions." Bobby raised his cup in a cheerful toast.

"Maybe a few hours ago," Ortega said. "Now it's more like the lunch of people that didn't even make the podium."

I studied Ortega's face. From his wry smile to the twinkle in his narrowed eyes, I didn't think he actually disapproved of my meal or my tardiness. But I found him hard to read, sometimes. "You brought these in?"

Ortega nodded. "They were fresh this morning. Markus is out of town, and I didn't think either of you would think to bring in bagels."

"I thought about it," Bobby said. "But then I drove past Noah's and came straight to the office. At least I made coffee."

"You got into my secret stash and put Kopi Luwak through the Mr. Coffee." Ortega's nostrils flared and his jaw clenched. No difficulty reading that.

Bobby brought his coffee cup to his lips and slurped. He kept his eyes forward, not looking at Ortega, the man we both ostensibly worked for.

"Did you want a cup?" Ortega asked, and then gestured towards the metal carafe on the counter.

"That's the stuff that goes through a cat first?"

"A civet, actually, but yes."

"I'll pass. Have ... uh ... either of you been on a jury before?"

"You got the summons?" Bobby asked.

I nodded.

"Bummer, man. It's okay, though. Listen. If you get called in, just tell them that you believe that the jury is the crucible in which laws are tested. Hit them hard with that Libertarian shit, and you'll get dismissed right away."

Ortega sighed. "Don't listen to Mr. Greenwood. It is our civic duty to serve."

"It's boring and a waste of your time, Mel. Trust me. Get out of it if you can."

• • •

A couple of days later, I called the number on the summons and a robot told me I needed to show up on Monday morning. I spent the weekend worrying about it while I tried to adjust my sleep schedule. Serving on the jury itself isn't such a big deal, but I had run-ins with the law. I had been a "person of interest" in a murder, which I think is just a fancy way of them saying I was the suspect. What if showing up brought all those legal headaches back to the surface? I didn't want to go to jail, and I didn't want to run and start over. Again.

Monday morning, I found myself in a long line waiting to check in and get a badge. The summons mentioned something about parking and lunch reimbursement, but I needed to conquer the long, shuffling line first. After getting scanned at the door and heading upstairs, the place felt like a business office, with unflattering ceiling lights, scuffed linoleum, and bureaucracy as far as the eye could see. The movies never show this part of the legal system. It's a grist mill designed to grind everyday folk like me into legal powder.

Hundreds of people showed up for jury duty. They ranged in age, coloration, class, and ethnicity. I looked at all the people clogging up waiting areas and sitting on benches, waiting to be called and assigned to a courtroom. Some came prepared with a book to read. Most played on their phone. I tried not to look too closely at any of them. I kept my natural eyes down and my mind's eye shut as I filled out the forms. Bobby was right. I just needed to wait out the day and get on with my life.

They started calling names. Alphabetically, of course, which meant I had a while before they got to mine.

"Walker, Melch ... Melchiz ..."

"Present," I said. No one ever pronounces my first name right, unless they're huge into Bible thumping.

I walked upstairs with about fifty other people and entered one of the courtrooms. For the first time that day, the experience started to feel more like what popular media promised. Wood paneled walls everywhere, with a heavyset, steely-eyed bailiff standing by, watching us all take our seats. The judge's seat sat empty and elevated on the other side of the room, beyond an open space. A wooden banister separated the court from the spectator seating.

And, of course, the jury box sat off to one side, raised but not quite as tall as the judge's desk.

The lawyers sat at tables on the other side of the banister, watching as all the prospective jurors filed in. The one on the right, a dark-skinned man with short hair, a thin mustache, and soft eyes, scanned the crowd with a neutral expression. The attorney on the left, a middle-aged woman with kinky blond hair, light skin, and wire-framed glasses, smiled at us.

I looked between them, uncertain which one I was supposed to root for. The man's dark gray suit looked crisp with sharp lines, which suited his air of confidence. The woman looked frumpy and maternal in a long brown skirt and off-white blouse. She reminded me of a teacher I had in fourth grade that used to unfairly keep me after school.

Jury duty involves a lot of waiting. We waited to check in, then we waited to get called, and then we waited in the courtroom for something to happen. In the courtroom, we waited in silence. I don't think we were explicitly told to be quiet, but the air was cool and heavy. People's lives were changed in that room, and it seemed perverse to turn to your neighbor and start chatting about the weather.

"It's a nice day for this, at least." A man to my left spoke to me.

I turned and looked at him, unable to respond. He wore a button-down, red and black plaid shirt that would have been right at home adorning a lumberjack if it had been made of flannel. A white man with silvering black hair, he held a battered 49ers baseball cap in his lap.

"Is this your first time?" the man asked.

I nodded, still not wanting to violate the solemnity of the room. Perhaps if I didn't speak, he would stop talking.

"It's nothing to worry about. They'll give very clear instructions. You're going to do fine up there."

I looked around the rest of the room. At least fifty other people shared the spectator benches with me. My eyes slid over to the jury box, with its twelve empty chairs. "I doubt I'll wind up in the box."

"Yeah, well. We'll see."

The door leading into the hall opened and a woman in a business suit strode in. She hurried to the banister, which the bailiff opened to let her through.

"Sorry!" she said. She took a seat at another desk with some equipment I hadn't seen before. Stenographer. It looked like a small typewriter, with the keys replaced with small organ pedals. She turned on the device, fiddled with it for a moment, then gave the bailiff a nod.

"All rise," the bailiff said.

Benches creaked and a few people grunted as we all climbed to our feet.

A door opened next to the judge's bench. It blended in so well with the wall that I hadn't seen it until it opened. An old white man, tall and thin, stepped out in black robes and approached his bench.

"The honorable Judge Gaimon presiding."

"Please be seated," Judge Gaimon said. He wore thin glasses and addressed the prospective jurors with a reedy voice. "Thank you for your patience, everyone. We have a little bit of administration to finish, but then we'll get started with the jury selection process called *voir dire*. You have already filled out a questionnaire which is part of the process, and a dozen of you will be brought up and seated to my left. Counsel for both the plaintiff and the defense will ask questions, and you may be dismissed by either of them, or myself. If you are dismissed, it is not a reflection of your character, and you're not in trouble. You may be dismissed for any reason and once dismissed, you are free to go, your duty served."

The judge continued speaking for a while, talking about the history of *voir dire* and what he expected the schedule to be like for the trial. I zoned out a little bit, trying to remember the exact words Bobby gave me. Something about being a Libertarian?

"Walker, Melchizedek."

I jumped. The bailiff had just called my name, and even pronounced my first name correctly. I spaced out and hadn't realized the judge stopped talking. I stood up, and the faces of all the strangers pinned me in place.

"Please move to the jury box and take the next seat as I call you," the bailiff continued. "Bottom first, then top. Tredder, Isiah."

I went to the end of the box and sat down. I listened as the bailiff called out more names, and more strangers stood and took seats in the box. They were picking people in reverse alphabetical order. Is this how they always did it, or had I come in on the wrong day?

Once the box was full, the judge addressed us. "We realize that serving on a jury can be a burden. If anyone currently seated in the box can think of a reason why they cannot serve, please rise and state your reasons at this time."

A young Hispanic woman with a bow in her hair stood up in my row. "Sir, you said this case could go for several weeks? I am a single mother and will not be able to get child care for that long."

The judge looked down at a page in front of him. "Ms. Vasquez? You're free to go. Thank you for your time."

Ms. Vasquez shuffled out of the box and left through the main door. Another juror, a white man about my age and sitting in the back of the box, stood up.

"Your honor, I'm in college and this is finals week."

Again, the judge looked down at his seating chart. "Mr. Dardano. Thank you for your time. You are excused, and good luck on your exams."

I stood up and blanked out. I wasn't entirely sure I remembered what Bobby told me to say, but if I gave the finals week excuse, maybe I could get out that way. But then again, if I got caught in the lie, that would be extraordinarily bad.

"Mr. Walker?" the judge asked.

"I'm ..." The lie curdled on my tongue, and I switched back to Bobby's excuse at the last moment. "I believe the law is a crucible which — no, the court is a crucible which —"

"Mr. Walker." The judge did not sound happy.

"Yes, sir?"

"Can you tell me what you think a crucible is?"

Of course I knew what a crucible was. I worked with a practicing witch that crafted elixirs and spell components. You put the material in the bowl and then crush it with the stone part. Or was that a mortar and pestle?

I paused just a little too long. The judge continued. "Do you think you can follow simple instructions as they are presented by this court?"

"Yes, sir."

"Then please sit down, Mr. Walker."

The *voir dire* continued. The attorneys asked questions based on the questionnaire, and several other people were dismissed. Prospective jurors were pulled up to fill the gaps, including the man with the 49ers cap. Twelve jurors in the box, plus two alternates sitting on chairs just outside the jury box.

They found no reason to dismiss me. That's how I became Juror Number One.

• • •

Not long after the jury was selected, they let us go for the day. The judge read several pages of instructions, talking about what "reasonable doubt" meant, what our responsibility as a jury would be, and what the schedule was expected to be like. He spent a great deal of time talking about "circumstantial evidence," what it means, and how, contrary to popular media, it is perfectly acceptable in a court of law. As this instruction was explained to us, we were each given a binder with blank paper in it and told we could write as many notes as we wanted. Several people around me began jotting things down immediately. I left mine blank, figuring if it comes down to a test, I'd just look off someone else's work.

When instructions were complete, I left the building and squinted against early afternoon sunlight. The courthouse sits around 8th and H street, while The Society's office is near 20th and K. A little bit of a walk, but not terrible. It gave me time to think.

Murder in the first degree. They had me, a psychic that can talk to ghosts, sitting as a juror in a murder case. Incredible.

I wasn't going to have to worry about "reasonable doubt." If they had the murder weapon and they let me touch it, I could pull a vision from it and tell them not only who the murderer was, but what they were thinking as they were doing it. I could give them all the details they could ever need. But the judge was very specific with his instructions: we were to determine if the defendant was guilty beyond a reasonable doubt based *only* on the evidence provided.

At The Society's office, I ran into Bobby. We were told not to talk about the case until it was over, but Bobby convinced me that it wouldn't hurt anything to let him know what was going on. He didn't really have any advice for me, and I didn't stay too long. When I let Ortega know that I'd be hung up on the jury for the next few weeks, he told me not to worry about Society work until the case was done. He didn't want me trying to deal with anything supernatural if I was going to be distracted. I took the light rail back to my trailer and played on my X-Box the rest of the evening.

The next morning in court, I sat in the jury box with my head in my hands as a headache pounded behind my eyes. I should have sent Master Chief to bed way earlier than I did, but adjusting one's sleep schedule is hard. On the first real day of the trial, I paid the price for my night-owl ways.

We did the "all rise" dance again, and the judge reiterated some of the instructions he gave us the day before. The repetition bordered on patronizing, but I figured they had to do it just to make sure even the dullest juror was on the same page. As the judge spoke, I studied the defendant.

David Gomez, an Hispanic man with half-lidded eyes and facial tattoos, sat next to the matronly attorney on the other side of the room from me. A cheap brown suit covered his body, but it would be overstating things to say he wore it. The sides of his head were shaved, with the rest of his hair long, and held back in a pony tail. He stared into the empty space in front of him.

I wanted to study him with my mind's eye open, but Ortega warned me against it. The justice system, he said, is imperfect, and innocent people die. Some of them linger on as angry but harmless spirits, and some of those might haunt the courthouse, the place where they were served injustice. If I opened my mind's eye, I might be able to read an aura off of the defendant, but any angry spirits in the area would see me and create complications.

"You have heard your instructions," the prosecuting attorney said, standing up. He wore a different suit than the first day, just as immaculate, but a lighter gray. His voice filled the room and entered my brain like ear candy. He could have read a phone book with that voice, and it would have been captivating. "Over the next few days, we will present evidence that will paint a clear picture of what happened on the night of January 16th when Anthony Woods lost his life.

"As you have been instructed, Mr. Gomez is to be presumed innocent until proven guilty. I encourage you to take this instruction seriously. The burden of proof is on me, not on Ms. Temple to prove Mr. Gomez innocent. It is a high burden, but after evidence is presented in this case, I am confident you will be convinced beyond a reasonable doubt that Mr. Gomez took the life of Mr. Woods, and that it was premeditated with malice aforethought.

"Some of the evidence that will be presented will be difficult to look at. You were all asked if images of a particularly grotesque or gory nature would be upsetting and make it difficult to make a fair and impartial decision. You all agreed, both verbally and on the questionnaire, that you could do this. When evidence is presented, do not look away.

"We will prove that Mr. Woods and Mr. Gomez had an altercation on the night before Mr. Woods was murdered. Testimony will be given by experts proving that we have the murder weapon, and that the murder weapon was held by Mr. Gomez. Police that arrived at the scene will give their testimony, describing how they found the defendant and the deceased, and they will give their account of what happened the night Mr. Woods was murdered. Thank you."

The prosecuting attorney sat down at his desk. Someone in the jury box sitting behind me coughed. The courtroom fell silent for several moments, save for the quiet clicking of the stenographer's machine. The prosecution's opening statement wasn't what I expected. He never walked around or approached the jury's box. There were no theatrics. I could not recall a movie or TV show that presented the workings of a courtroom quite like this.

"Good morning, everyone." The defense attorney, Ms. Temple, stood up. The frail lilt to her voice further reminded me of that grade school teacher that hated me all those years ago. "Mr. Parker's opening statement is correct, in that my client, David Gomez, must be presumed innocent until proven guilty. The prosecution must prove beyond a reasonable doubt that my client did this terrible crime. It will be especially challenging for Mr. Parker to prove these things as Mr. Gomez is innocent.

"You have been given instructions regarding circumstantial evidence. Mr. Parker will lay this out and try to tell you a story supported by this circumstantial evidence. You have all received handouts that give an example of this. It talks about seeing a man drenched head to toe. One reasonable explanation is that he was caught outside in the rain without an umbrella. The water soaking the man is circumstantial evidence, and without any other information, it is a reasonable conclusion. But what if you find out that he's a plumber, and he was scheduled to work that day? Now there is reasonable doubt as to whether or not the rain was involved at all.

"That's what this case will come down to. Mr. Parker will provide an explanation for the evidence, and will tell you that Mr. Gomez is guilty of killing Mr. Woods. But is it the only reasonable explanation? This will come down to the quality of the evidence, which upon examination, will not be sufficient to overcome the presumption of innocence of Mr. Gomez. Thank you."

The judge asked the prosecution something, and Mr. Parker responded. Words were exchanged between the judge and both sets of lawyers, which sounded like a ritual to me. Mr. Parker had a chance to rebut Ms. Temple. Both sides were done with their opening statements.

"The prosecution may call their first witness," said Judge Gaimon. The real show was about to begin.

• • •

The first witness called was a police sergeant. A bailiff —I didn't realize until that moment that there were more than one — stepped out into the hall, then returned with a cop in full uniform. He walked with heavy footfalls that filled the chamber with percussive taps. Young and in-shape, he still had his radio clipped to his shoulder and his gun strapped to his hip. He took the witness stand and the court clerk swore him in.

"Officer Vann," Mr. Parker said, his voice as smooth and silky as ever. "Can you please recall where you were and what you were doing on the evening of January 16th of this year? Specifically from around 9 p.m. and onward."

"Around 9 p.m., my partner and I were northbound on Watt, approaching North Highlands. My partner was driving, and I was a little distracted. We had an ROTC student with an interest in becoming an MP doing a ride-along, and I was answering questions."

"Is that when you were called to respond to a situation taking place at Diablo Park?"

"That's right. We were the closest, so we acknowledged the call, turned down Elkhorn, and proceeded to the park."

"What did you find at the scene?"

"At the southern end of the park on the sidewalk, there was a body on the ground. It was dark, but in the headlights we could see that they were bleeding. There was someone else running away from the body, north along the park."

"What did you do?"

"My partner, Officer Lewis, pulled the car over and called for an ambulance. I hopped out of the car and pursued the one fleeing the scene of the crime."

"Did you catch them?"

"Yes, sir."

"It sounds like they had quite a head start on you.

Were you a track star, Officer Vann? How did you manage to catch the assailant?"

"Objection," Ms. Temple said. "The use of the word 'assailant' implies guilt that has not been proven."

"I'll rephrase," Mr. Parker said. "Officer Vann, how did you catch the individual fleeing the scene of the crime?"

Officer Vann cleared his throat. "It was dark. The sidewalk along the park winds around, and there are these knee-high posts along the edge of the concrete. It looked like he clipped one of his legs on a post and went down."

"The person tripped and you were able to apprehend them. Can you identify the person you caught fleeing the scene of the crime?"

Officer Vann pointed at David Gomez. "That's him, sitting with the defense."

"The witness has identified the defendant," Mr. Parker said, addressing the stenographer. "Did Mr. Gomez put up any kind of resistance?"

"No, sir."

"Did you handcuff him?"

"Yes, sir."

"Did he have anything in his hands when you handcuffed him?"

"He had a knife."

Mr. Parker opened a cardboard box decorated with yellow and black tape along the top. He held up a clear plastic bag containing what looked like a hunting knife. "Is this the weapon that you retrieved from Mr. Gomez?"

Officer Vann narrowed his eyes. "Yeah, that looks like it."

"Did Mr. Gomez say or do anything once you placed him under arrest?"

"No, sir. He followed all instructions given to him, meek as a lamb."

"Thank you, Officer Vann. Your Honor, I have no further questions for this witness at this time."

Ms. Temple stood and asked some clarifying questions. She asked if the witness saw Mr. Gomez with the victim, which Officer Vann denied. It didn't really matter. The picture the cop painted was pretty clear. I looked at David Gomez, sitting quietly in his ill-fitting suit, and wondered how this case was supposed to last for weeks. It seemed like we could have this wrapped up this afternoon.

• • •

They let us go early, not because the case wrapped up, but because a couple of witnesses were not available as planned. I went home thinking about David Gomez, and how he sat so quiet through the proceedings, not really looking at anyone. Is that how guilt affects a person? Or was Gomez special in some way?

The next day established a pattern that continued on into the next week. I got up early, took the light rail downtown with my laminated jury badge in my pocket. Once in the courthouse, I got in line to pass through a security line that would have been right at home at the airport. On the other side of the scanner, I clipped my badge to my shirt and went up to the courtroom where a couple of other early jurors waited to be let in.

Once inside, we took our seats in the box, picked up our notebooks, and listened while the lawyers summoned the next set of witnesses and put them to the question. There was a forensic expert that was able to state with a high level of confidence that the weapon recovered from David Gomez was the one used to kill Anthony Woods. There was a coroner that testified, describing in nauseating detail how Woods died shortly after the police arrived. Officer Lewis, the driver, came in and gave a nearly identical testimony as his partner, Officer Vann.

One day, a bailiff wheeled in a large screen. Mr. Parker used it to show us pictures of the victim. Some of the pictures were close-ups of the stab wound, which were disgusting, but nothing worse than anything I've seen in a decent horror movie. We had to take a short break after that, though, as the images made Juror Number Nine sick.

Mr. Parker also showed us pictures of the scene of the crime, both at night and the next day. The pictures weren't that interesting, other than the bloodstains on the concrete, but I sat up and paid attention. I recognized the area. Diablo Park wasn't that far away from the cemetery where my friend Kate was buried.

Mr. Parker spent a week and a half building his case, stacking evidence on top of the premise he laid out in his opening statement. Images often accompanied the witness testimonies, so we didn't have to rely on our imagination.

Ms. Temple, the defense attorney, sometimes asked clarifying questions of witnesses, or occasionally made minor objections to the way Mr. Parker worded his questions. Other than that, she seemed unable to stop the torrent of facts that damned her client.

Mr. Parker remained silky smooth. Ms. Temple smiled congenially and jotted notes on a legal pad. And Gomez sat still and silent as a headstone while the prosecution meticulously and thoroughly sealed his fate.

He didn't appear to be without supporters, but if that gave him any comfort, I couldn't tell from looking at him. Just as the jury showed up every day to quietly sit and listen to the evidence, a handful of people sat in the audience, dressed in clothes that looked more appropriate to Gomez than the ill-fitting suits Ms. Temple dressed him in. These were people my age or maybe a little younger, wearing t-shirts and ripped jeans. When they weren't wearing sunglasses, I could see darkness around their eyes that may or may not have been mascara or eyeliner. They sat behind Gomez, their goth eyes boring holes in the back of his head.

Mr. Parker called his last witness, a waitress from a place called Billiards. She looked about the same age as Gomez, or maybe a little bit older, dressed in jeans and a faded Metallica t-shirt. I appreciated how normal she dressed; all of the other witnesses wore either a police uniform or a business suit or dress.

"For the record, please state your name," said the court clerk.

"Gwen Oliver."

"And where do you currently work, Ms. Oliver?"

The witness drew in a deep breath and the corners of her mouth turned down before she answered. "I'm a server at Billiards, at Garfield and Auburn."

"Were you working a shift there on the evening of January 15th?"

Gwen smirked. "That was many months ago, but yes, I remember working there that night."

"What makes that night so memorable to you?"

"Aside from the police and lawyers asking me about it repeatedly?"

"Yes, Ms. Oliver, what happened during your shift at Billiards on the evening of January 15th?"

"David and Tony got in an argument."

"And when you said 'David and Tony' you mean —"

"I mean David Gomez, sitting right over there, and Tony Woods, the guy that died the next night."

"Do you recall what the argument was about?"

"No, I don't know what it was about. David shoved Tony and yelled, 'You idiot! You're fucking dead,' and then he stormed out. But that —"

"Thank you, Ms. Oliver. Your honor, I have no more questions for the witness at this time."

"Ms. Temple?" the judge asked in his reedy voice.

The defense attorney stood up. She either wore the same drab brown skirt and blouse as previous days, or something similar enough that it looked the same to me. She smiled her best teacher's smile as she addressed Gwen. "You were trying to say something there at the end. Would you like to say it now?"

"Objection, hearsay," said Mr. Parker.

"Sustained."

Ms. Temple nodded. "Ms. Oliver, did you know David Gomez and Anthony Woods personally?"

"Yeah."

"Did you notice them get into arguments like that before?"

"No."

"How many times had you seen them together?"

"More times than I could count. They were there all the time. They acted like brothers."

Ms. Temple paused for several moments, her brow furrowed. She gave Mr. Parker a long look before turning to the judge. "I have no more questions for this witness at this time, but reserve the right to call her again."

As the witness was excused, I leaned back in my seat and studied David Gomez. He continued to sit in silence, staring at nothing in front of him. For the first time since the case began, a slim doubt shadowed my mind. The prosecution called a witness to establish the defendant's state of mind before the murder, and that witness seemed to want to come to David Gomez's defense. After all the other evidence put before us, it made me wonder why.

• • •

As I sat on the light rail watching the Sacramento streets streak by, the seed of doubt began to grow. Prosecution provided a reason why Gomez killed Woods. They had some kind of falling out, argued the night before, and Gomez was heard threatening Woods's life. But why? What makes someone so angry that they turn around and kill their best friend the next day?

We were given explicit instructions not to visit the scene of the crime. In fact, we weren't supposed to consider anything but the evidence presented inside the court. No Internet searches. No diving into old newspaper articles. Only the evidence presented either by Mr. Parker or Ms. Temple.

But it had been months since Tony Woods died, and the murder took place at a public park. It's not like there would still be police tape or investigators snooping over the place. If I got off at Watt and hopped on the 80, I could be wandering around the park myself, with no one the wiser for it.

So I did. Sometimes I drive faster than the posted speed limit. Sometimes I cross the street when I'm not at a crosswalk. And if it's against the law to visit the scene of the crime while serving as a juror, well, I guess I do that sometimes, too.

A short walk down Diablo from Elkhorn, I found the place Mr. Parker showed us in those pictures. A long, thin park, it had a community center and large parking lot on one side of the street, and a long, narrow patch of grass and a walking path on the other. Like so much of the rest of Sacramento, numerous trees reached for the sky, providing long shadows as the sun began to set.

A couple of people played tennis in the courts across the street. An older man with long, graying hair walked their dog along the path. Cars rolled up and down Diablo. Plenty of people shared the park with me, and none of them appeared to take an interest in me or give me a second thought.

Comfortably alone at the place where Woods was murdered, I opened my mind's eye. Shadows faded, and the world became clear and crisp, a sort of hyper-reality filling my mind in place of the vision my physical eyes provided. I turned in a slow circle. I didn't see any ghosts. Nothing stood out to me, and none of the people occupying the park wore any of the many auras that indicated a supernatural connection.

Tony Woods didn't haunt the place, so I couldn't talk to him about what happened. If I was going to see what happened the night someone stuck a knife in his chest, I was going to need to look back across the span of time and see for myself. I was going to have to do this the hard way.

I have always had difficulty describing what it's like when I look back across time. Standing there in the park,

I turned to my right, without turning my body. With my natural eyes, I could still see the world in the present, with shadows at my feet and leaves gently wafting in the gentle Sacramento delta winds. On top of that, I saw a reflection of the world as it once was, moving backwards, like hitting rewind on an old video.

When I first learned to do this, I couldn't look back more than a month or so. The present pulls on me, making it harder and harder to rewind time. These days, I can turn back time a year or more. The challenge is keeping track of how far back I'm looking. It's not like I can look at a watch and figure it out. I have to count the number of times the sun transits the sky.

I looked up at the sky and through my mind's eye, watched the sun rise in the west and set in the east, as fast as I could make it roll backwards. It helped to look up when I did this. Watching the people race through the space could be distracting at best, nauseating at its worst, whereas the clouds whipping across the sky was kind of pretty.

With each regressing day, I tapped my finger against my thigh. On the way to Diablo Park, Google told me it had been 244 days since January 16th. Even counting by fives and tens, it was easy to lose track, and I didn't want to start over if I didn't have to.

At 200 days backwards, I heard footsteps crunching on the walkway coming towards me. I paused the turning at 205, feeling the pull of the present hard enough to make sweat bead on my brow and along my spine. I flicked my eyes towards the approaching individual and wished I hadn't. A cop, with one hand on their belt, the other hovering near the radio clipped to their shoulder. More sweat dampened my shirt, which had nothing to do with trying to look back across the boundaries of time.

"You okay, buddy?" The cop asked. He was white, with close-cropped black hair. While it would be overstating things to describe him as fat, his round cheeks and puffed out chest made me think of him as "fleshy."

"Oh, yeah, I'm fine." I concentrated on not letting my vision slip. At the same time, I tried to think of a good reason for me to be standing there. They caught me visiting the scene of the crime. Were they going to send me to jail? Again?

"You just look like you might be a little bit out of it. Do you need me to call someone for you?"

Think, think, think. And focus. I could try to stand up for my right to be there, but cops generally hate that, especially when you're right. Best case scenario, he would keep asking me questions and leave me alone, but not before I lost focus, which would lead to starting over. Worst case scenario, he'd pack me off for a drug or alcohol test, saying something about me being drunk or disorderly in public.

No, I just needed to give him a good lie. If only I had one. "No, thanks. My phone still has a charge."

"Are you sure you're feeling well? You're sweating like you've been running a marathon."

I felt my grip on the vision slip a little. I set my jaw and focused on the clouds again. My brain raced, trying to think of some excuse. "Uhm ... it's like this."

"Yeah?"

"You know that Starbucks down the street, at the corner on Elkhorn?"

"Yeah, I just came from there."

"I think their cake pops have coconut in them or something. I'm allergic."

"Oh, man. Do you need me to get you an EpiPen? Call an ambulance?" The cop picked up his radio.

I hadn't thought through the ramifications of that particular lie, but there was no going back now. "Nah, man, it's not that bad. Please don't get an ambulance. My insurance sucks, and I just need to wait this out."

"Are you sure?"

"Yeah. If I just hang out here for a few, it will pass."

"Okay, man. I'll wait here with you, and if you change your mind, just say the word." He paused long enough to press the button on his radio. "Possible ten-fifty-six. Standing by."

Having the cop hanging around might make things awkward, depending on where Woods was stabbed, but that couldn't be helped. I continued turning back time, counting sunrises and doing my best to ignore the cop.

Once I reached my count, I slowed down and looked towards the street. Phantom cars whizzed by, their lights cutting through a night that took place most of a year ago. I kept pushing back fairly fast, until the red and blue lightbars of an emergency vehicle blurred by. I blew right past the murder, but at least I found the right evening.

I rolled my shoulders and relaxed my grip on the vision, allowing it to slide towards the present. "I think I'm starting to feel better already."

"That's good to hear." The cop sounded genuinely relieved, but he didn't leave.

I let the vision slip forward a bit faster. Even though I was looking for Woods, expecting to see him, my heart still skipped a beat when he appeared on the sidewalk. He turned into the park, the hood of his coat up and his hands tucked in his pockets as he made his way to a stone bench beneath the trees.

Another man waited there, sitting on the back of the bench, smoking either a joint or a cigarette. They were far enough away it was difficult to tell which, and with the cop watching me, I didn't dare move deeper into the park to check.

Woods and the stranger exchanged words which I couldn't hear. Even if I had been standing right next to them, I wouldn't have heard anything. Being able to look back through time allows me to see the past, not hear it. According to Ortega, some psychics could hear without seeing, or look into the future instead of the past. It would have been nice to know what they were arguing about, but it really didn't matter, as long as I could see the face of the murderer. I knew Gomez did it. I just needed to see.

The argument turned into a fight. Woods drove a fist deep into the stomach of the hooded figure. They both fell onto the bench and rolled. I watched from a distance, my heart racing. I knew how this fight would end. They showed us the pictures in court. But I couldn't help myself. Both men were strangers to me, yet I hoped Woods would somehow come out on top and get away.

The hooded man brought a knee up into Woods' groin. Woods crumpled, and the hooded figure got up. He pushed Woods onto the bench and punched him in the face. Then again. Woods lay there, his arms hanging limp to his side. The hooded figure reached into his sweater, pulled out his knife, and held it high. He hesitated. I held my breath, and I paused the flow of time. I wanted Gomez to change his mind. Woods was beaten. It was his best friend. He didn't need to die.

I steeled myself and let the vision continue. Gomez brought the knife down hard, stabbing Woods in the chest. The blade sunk into his flesh to the hilt. Gomez held Woods like that for a while, looking into his face. Maybe he was saying something. I couldn't tell. I still hadn't seen the murderer's face.

The hooded figure released the knife and stood straight. He brushed himself off, turned around, and started walking towards me. This hadn't played out quite like I imagined. Where were the cops? Gomez left the knife behind. Didn't the cop say in court that he ran him down and pulled the knife out of his hands?

He got close enough for me to see inside his hood, and I froze the vision once again. My heart thudded hard in my chest. I recognized the face.

"It's not Gomez," I said.

"What was that?"

The cop was still with me, in the present. I was so wrapped up in the vision, I lost track of what was going on around me. I closed my mind's eye and let the vision drop. I'd seen enough.

I turned to the cop. "I'm good. I'm going to go catch the bus, now."

"You sure you're okay? You look worse than when I first got here. Let me take you to the hospital."

"No, thank you." I walked past the cop, giving him a wide berth.

The cop said something into his radio, and I ignored him. I kept walking, not too fast, back to the sidewalk and up the street. After a few steps I looked back. The cop kept his eyes on me but remained where he stood. Good. The last thing I needed was another entanglement with the legal system.

I had a big enough problem in front of me to deal with. David Gomez did not kill Anthony Woods. And he and I might be the only ones in the world that knew the truth.

• • •

The defense made their case. Ms. Temple did not have the gravitas of Mr. Parker, and she also didn't have the witnesses. She called a forensics expert that specialized in fingerprints. The expert found lots of prints on the handle of the knife, but none of them were definitive matches to anyone, including Gomez. Ms. Temple also called a coroner. She asserted that to bleed out from the kind of wounds Woods received, it would take at least an hour.

I watched David Gomez. An innocent man in a cheap, ill-fitting suit. He continued to sit there silent and meek. Ms. Temple never called him to the stand. How could he sit there still and quiet while his future was irrevocably ruined by a court that seemed determined to hold to a lie?

The worst part was that the actual murderer was there the whole time. He sat behind Gomez with the other goth kids, staring at the back of Gomez's head, his lips twisted into a smirk. Thin, with tattoos crawling up his neck, and hair cut down to peach fuzz, there was no doubt in my mind. This was the one I saw. The one that beat Woods down, plunged a knife in his chest, then just walked away.

I couldn't say anything. Who would I tell, and what would I say? My stomach turned over and over, acid crawling up and giving me heartburn the longer the case went. The longer Ms. Temple failed to put up any meaningful defense.

On the last morning of the trial, I woke up and lay in my bed, staring at my laminated badge. On the back, there was a number I could call in case of an emergency or illness. If I called and told them I was sick, it wouldn't be a complete lie. They told us the day before that they expected it to be the last day, and I had not slept well. I didn't know how I was going to go in and watch an innocent man get prosecuted for murder. There were two spare jurors that sat outside the jury box every day, taking notes like the rest of us. If I called in sick, one of them would take my place, and I would be free.

David Gomez would go to jail, and it wouldn't have anything to do with me.

I couldn't do it, though. I forced myself out of bed, took a cold shower, and made my way to the light rail. By the time I set foot in the courtroom, I knew I made the right decision. I don't think I could have lived with myself if I took the coward's way out.

Before I knew what was going on, they ushered the jury through a set of doors, down a hallway, and into a small conference room. We sat at two folding tables pushed together. Maria, the young Hispanic woman I only knew as "Juror Number Seven," folded a piece of paper into a triangle and put her name in front of her. The other jurors followed her lead with varying levels of success at folding name tags.

"The first thing we need to do is select a foreman," Maria said, holding up a blank form. "It doesn't matter how we do it. We just need to put their name on the form, and they'll be responsible for filling out forms and answering the judge after we find our verdict."

Naturally, we selected Maria to be our foreman. Juror Number Nine, a white stay-at-home Mom named Susan, with a perpetually sour expression, like everything would be better if she could just speak to the manager, voiced interest in being foreman. When it came out that Maria studied law, even Susan agreed that Maria was the best choice.

"Let's start with a quick vote and see if there is anything for us to deliberate," Maria said. "If you believe that the defendant is guilty, raise your hand."

Everyone raised their hand except me.

"That was easy," said Juror Number Eight, an older man named James according to his name tag. He was the same man that spoke to me before we were selected to be on the jury. His battered 49ers cap sat on the table next to his name tag.

Juror Number Eleven, Jennifer, nodded with James, as did Number Three, Jared. I looked around the table. There were quite a few people with first names that started with a J.

"Hold on," Maria said, looking at me. "Mel, do you believe the defendant is not guilty?"

"I don't believe he killed his best friend, no," I said.

"Oh shit, here we go," said Juror Number Two. Isiah. Another white man, my age or a little older, he wore a plain black t-shirt which exposed a series of poorly drawn tattoos running up his right arm.

"He's just looking to waste our time," Susan said, looking at Maria.

"I'd like to hear his reasoning," said Juror Number Six. Juan. Something about his features reminded me of a younger version of Pedro Ortega.

"Same," said Juror Number Four. An older black man named Francis.

The table went silent and eleven sets of eyes tried to stare me down. I felt a line of sweat run down my back, but my voice was steady when I spoke. "There are details that just don't line up for me."

"Which details?" Juror Number Five, a short white man named Carry, with a pinched face beneath coke-bottle glasses. He opened his binder in front of him, revealing pages and pages of handwritten notes.

"The coroner said that it would take hours for the victim to bleed out, right?"

Carry turned to a page towards the back of the binder. "Not hours. They said, 'At least an hour.'"

"Okay, fine. So the prosecution's case is that David Gomez plunged a knife into his best friend and then, what? Just hung out at the park for an hour?"

"I'm changing my vote," Juan said.

"Oh, come on!" Jared said. "The defense brought in a scientist that gave an opinion that fit their needs. If anyone should be changing their vote, it should be Mel, so we can be done with this."

"I'd like to hear more," Carry said, pushing his glasses up his nose.

I looked around the room again. Juror Number Ten, a college student named Mitch, still hadn't said anything. His mouth hung open, and a slight frown furrowed his brow as he looked around the table.

Juror Number Twelve, another one we hadn't heard from, kept looking towards Maria. His name tag marked him as Jeff, another J name. He also wore glasses, though not as heavy as Carry's. I had a hard time reading his expression.

I turned and looked at Isiah. One of his tattoos caught my attention. I tilted my head to read it a little better. The letters A, C, and A went up his arm, his sleeve possibly hiding a fourth letter. If he hated cops enough to permanently write it on his skin, I might be able to use that.

"Which do you trust more," I said, "the word of a scientist, or the testimony of a cop?"

Isiah sneered. He met my gaze and held it a moment before nodding.

Deliberations continued like that for another hour. After Juan switched his vote to innocent, Isiah, Carry, and Francis did the same. Carry was a lock after reiterating that the fingerprint information was inconclusive. Francis, who was always Francis and never Frank, seemed to like me and was ready to vote however I voted. From some things he said, I think I reminded him of his grandson.

Then there were the others. Most seemed to have an open mind, but they were still leaning towards guilt. Even Jared, as much as he blustered about getting it done and over with, seemed willing to agree that not all of the evidence fit quite as well as Mr. Parker presented it. The only jury member unwilling to give any ground was James, the man with the battered cap.

Maria ran us through a couple more votes, one of which was with paper ballots. In that vote, it came up split, 6 to 6.

"Uhm ..." Mitch said. "Isiah? You said that you don't trust the cops, and I get it. Cops suck. But I gotta be honest, I kinda stopped paying attention after that first day. They made it sound like that dude did it, and that was that. If the cops are wrong, then what happened that night?"

Isiah frowned, and I watched him. He didn't have an answer, and his face started to turn red. If I didn't say something, I knew he would flip again, ACAB be damned.

The problem was that I didn't have the full answer. I knew who killed Woods. I watched them do it. But I had no way of explaining who the murderer was, or what David Gomez was doing there.

"Maria," I said. "We're allowed to look at the evidence, right?"

"You want to look at something?"

"The murder weapon. Just for a moment."

"How is that going to help?" James asked.

"I just want to see it. I don't see how it will hurt."

Maria talked to the guard and a few minutes later, one of the bailiffs brought in the evidence box containing the knife and set the box in the middle of the table. I stood up, opened the box, and touched the knife through the plastic bag.

At first, I started to pull a vision from the bag itself. The most significant event involving the bag was when someone, bored and slightly hung-over, opened the bag and carefully slid the knife inside, even though their hands wanted to shake and they really needed something to steady themselves. Not particularly useful, as visions go.

I pinched the blade more tightly through the plastic, and there it was. It felt like a charge of electricity, straining to move up my arm and into my brain. The plastic didn't matter. The vision, strong and imposing, wanted to be seen. I held it at bay.

A vision that strong would have to be the murder itself. If I let it take me over, I would ride behind the eyes of the murderer. I would feel their feelings and think their thoughts, and I would feel the knife parting the flesh of Tony Woods. The thrill of the act would rush over me, and adrenaline would pump through my veins, just as it filled the murderer's.

I resisted the vision and looked for another. I didn't need more information about the killer. I already knew his face. Even knowing his motivation wouldn't help me, in that moment. I needed to find the less significant event in this knife's existence. The moment David Gomez pulled the knife from his best friend, Anthony Woods.

*"No, no, no." David knelt next to T. Blood oozed from beneath the knife, warm and sticky. It smelled like his Uncle's shop, when he still had that old metal lathe.*

*T didn't move. It looked like he dragged himself a short distance. Red stained leaves marked a trail going deeper into the park. T moved before he got there, but he wasn't moving now.*

*"Stay with me, man." David wiped tears from his eyes before wrapping his fingers around the hilt of the knife and pulling. The knife resisted, stuck in T's chest. David pulled again, harder this time. It wouldn't budge. T didn't move or react.*

*Why did he do it? It wasn't his fight. It wasn't his girl. We all knew Ellis was crazy. Even Kaley knew. Kaley especially knew. That's why she came to David in the first place. Fucking T. Why did you have to play hero?*

*David yanked harder on the knife, and it came free. There was more blood. Blood everywhere. It was on the knife. On his hands. Everywhere.*

*Sirens. Getting closer. And he was holding the knife.*

*No choice but to run. Damn it, T, why couldn't you keep your stupid mouth shut?*

I let the knife drop back in the box and covered my face with both hands. I could feel the eyes staring at me, all around, but I needed to take a moment. I didn't think tears were going to help me plead David's case.

"Mel?" Francis asked, his grandfatherly voice gentle.

"I'm okay." I took another moment to get my voice and my breathing under control. Separating my own emotions from that of David Gomez was not easy, but for his sake and for the sake of the deceased, I pushed through. I raised my head. "Mitch, you're looking for a different explanation for what happened that night, right?"

"Yeah."

"T ... Tony Woods ... went to the park that night to meet someone, but it wasn't David Gomez. It was probably about the thing that he and David argued about the night before. Tony met whoever he was meeting at the park. The other guy stabbed him, then walked away.

"About an hour later, long enough for Tony to bleed out, David showed up. Maybe he was late, I don't know. He found his best friend on the ground, a knife in his chest, and he pulled it out.

"That's when the cops showed up. David tried to run, because who wouldn't in that situation? But then he tripped, just like the cops said, and then they brought him in."

"No one in the courtroom said anything about someone else at the park," James said.

"We have to make our decision based on the evidence presented in the courtroom," Maria said.

"We're not looking for who did it," Jared said. "We're here to determine if the defendant did it. If he didn't, then someone else must have."

My mouth dropped open, and I stared at Jared. After everything he'd said about just getting this over with, he was the last person I expected to come to David's defense.

James tore out a piece of paper from his notebook and scribbled a note on it. He slid it across the table to me, then rose and headed for the door.

"James?" Maria asked. "Where are you going?"

"I gotta see a man about a horse."

Confused looks bloomed across the faces of all of us younger jurors.

"He means he's going to the bathroom," Francis said.

I looked at the note.

*Wait a couple minutes, then meet me in the bathroom.*

I stood up, crossed the room to one of the windows, and lifted one of the blinds. Below, I could see the main parking area for the courthouse. It was mostly empty, which made it easy for me to spot the murderer, standing next to his car. Ellis. The vision from the knife gave me a name to put to the face.

"I gotta pee, too," I said, and headed for the door.

Two steps into the bathroom, James stepped from behind the door and grabbed my arm.

"Hey!" I said.

"I know what you are," James said, his voice just above a whisper. The acoustics of the bathroom gave his words an echo, just the same.

I shrugged my arm out of his grip and took a step away from him. "Yeah? And what is that?"

"A psychic. Don't try to deny it. I saw it when you touched the knife."

There is nothing prohibiting me from telling people my secret. Bobbie, one of my friends in The Society, publicly pretends to do what I can do, and he makes money from it. I don't have to keep it a secret, but I do, because I figured out the hard way that most people really don't want to believe in the supernatural. It upsets them, and then *I* start to upset them, just by being around.

Looking in the eyes of the older man in front of me, all my practiced lies died in my throat. If this guy believed in psychics, then maybe I could change his vote by just being honest. "I got a vision of the person that murdered Tony. It wasn't David Gomez."

James swallowed, and his face went pale. "You're absolutely certain?"

I sighed. "I went to the scene of the crime and looked into the past. I saw it then. And just now, I pulled a vision from the knife. The guy's name is Ellis, and he's been in the courtroom every-"

"What you're saying is that there is no way you're going to let an innocent man hang for this."

"That's one way to put it, yes."

James drew in a deep breath and let it out slowly, puffing out his cheeks as he did so. His cheeks still looked pale, and there was still a tightness around his eyes, but when he spoke, his voice sounded cheery. "Okay, Mel. You win. Let's go back and wrap this up."

We returned to the deliberation room, and before I knew it, we had our decision. Susan seemed willing to vote whichever way Maria voted, and Jennifer was ready to follow James. Once James made it clear that he changed his mind, the rest of the holdouts followed suit.

Maria filled out the form and passed it to the bailiff. We were ushered back into the courtroom, into the jury box, and then we went through what seemed like a ritual ending to the case. The judge asked if we had come to a decision, and Maria delivered the answer.

For the first time, I saw genuine emotion fill the face of David Gomez. His eyes widened, his mouth dropped open, and then he lowered his face into his hands, presumably to hide the tears. He remained that way for several minutes. Ms. Temple rubbed his shoulders and spoke quietly in his ear, but it didn't seem to console David at all.

I did it. I used my gift to help keep an innocent man from facing penalties for a crime he did not commit. Why, then, did I have this nagging feeling that something bad was about to happen?

• • •

The judge thanked us for serving our duty and dismissed us. I hopped to my feet and walked out. Down the hall, near the stairs, I bent over a drinking fountain and splashed water into my face before taking a few, unsatisfying sips. The water was warm, and a little bit gritty.

"Heading home?" James stood behind me, his 49ers cap on his head.

"Eventually. I'm already downtown. I'll probably stop by the office first."

"Oh? Where do you work?"

I cocked my head as I looked into James' face. The shadow from the cap hid his eyes and made the lines of his cheeks sinister. "It's more like a consultant gig, actually."

James cast a quick glance at his watch. "We have a few minutes. Why don't you come to the cafeteria with me and get some coffee?"

"What do you mean, 'we have a few —'"

"Just come on. It'll be my treat."

James headed for the stairs and I followed. I'm not sure why. Curiosity motivated me, certainly, but there was something else, too. A nagging feeling I couldn't shake.

We found the cafeteria nearly deserted. They still had coffee out, and true to his word, James bought a cup for each of us. We took seats near one of the windows. The afternoon sunlight pouring in made the surface of the table painfully bright.

"First things first," James said. "Whatever happens next, it's not your fault."

"What?"

"You're going to blame yourself. Whatever I say, it won't matter. But maybe if I tell you now, it'll make it easier for you to see that you did nothing wrong."

"What are you talking about?"

"Mel, open your mind's eye and look at me."

The glare of the sunlight diminished, and the shadows disappeared. With my mind's eye open, I could see James' face clearly, in spite of the ball cap. An older man, with a weary smile and tears in his eyes.

Then a halo of light bloomed around James' head. He opened *his* mind's eye.

"Holy shit," I said.

"You see the past, right?"

"Yeah. Do you know Pedro Ortega? You should-"

"We don't have time for that, Mel. You see the past. I see the future."

"No shit?" I leaned forward in my seat. I couldn't help it. I loved my gift, don't get me wrong, but I can't tell you how many times I wished I could look the other way across time.

"It's not as awesome as you might think." James paused to wipe a tear from his eye. "The future isn't set. Not exactly. I see things that are possible. Sometimes things that are probable. And if I'm really lucky, sometimes I can change things so that disasters don't happen."

"What's about to happen, James?"

"Someone's going to die. Today. Soon."

"Who?"

"We'll get to that. When we got to deliberations, I knew one thing was for sure. Unless we found David Gomez guilty, someone would have to die."

"What? How does that-"

"Look, it doesn't matter anymore, right? Remember what I said at the beginning. What happens next isn't your fault."

"Who the fuck is going to die, James?"

"David Gomez." James took a long sip from his cup.

"When? Where?"

James looked at his watch. "Downstairs. On the street. You have just enough time to finish your cup."

I shook my head. It was all too much to accept. I wanted to process the idea that David Gomez was predicted to die, but I still needed to chew on the fact that another psychic sat across from me, one with a gift for the future. "Do you know about The Society of Supernatural Investigations?"

"I know who they are."

"You should let me introduce you. We could really use someone like you."

"I'll pass. Every member of your little group is associated with some unexplained death. I wouldn't fit in."

"Ouch." I drained half my cup.

"Okay, time to go."

"You said I had time to finish?"

"I was wrong. Let's move!"

We moved. I started for the elevator, but James grabbed my elbow and steered me towards the stairs.

"Too slow," James said. "Double time, now!"

James opened the door to the stairs for me and I took them two and three at a time. When I reached the bottom, I breathed hard. James came down right behind me, one hand on his chest and his cheeks red.

"Keep going," he wheezed.

I departed the stairwell and headed for the door. Not too fast; running past guards and cops is how you get the wrong kind of attention. Unless ... maybe we should get the police involved? I turned and looked back at James.

James didn't say anything. He shook his head and pointed to the door. He moved behind me at a quick walk, matching my own hurried pace. I took the hint. No cops.

I went outside and hurried down the short flight of stairs leading up to the courthouse. I looked around. At the intersection to my left, I saw a familiar car. A rusted yellow Mustang. A '96 or a '97, I couldn't tell. I last saw it from above, from the deliberation room. The tinted windows hid the driver from my vantage, but I could imagine Ellis inside, scowling and gripping the steering wheel with the same hands that killed Tony Wood. He was in the right turn lane on I Street, so when the light changed, he would pass on the street in front of me.

To my right, David Gomez walked towards the intersection at H Street. I didn't need James' gift to see what was about to happen. Ellis got away with murder once already. He'd try it again, with a car instead of a knife.

"David!" I shouted. I raised my hand and waved at him as I jogged in his direction.

David turned at the sound of his name and frowned at me. He bent his knees and half-turned away, ready to run. I slowed down and threw my friendliest smile at him. I didn't know what I was going to say, but it didn't matter. If I kept him from the intersection long enough, Ellis would drive by and everything would be okay.

"Do I know you?" David asked.

I stopped a few feet in front of him. "My name's Mel. I ... uh ... was on your jury."

Tires squealed behind me. I turned. The yellow mustang raced down the street and turned towards us. I could see Ellis's face through the windshield. His lips peeled back from gritted teeth. The engine roared. The front tires hit the curb, the bumper slammed into a gray fire hydrant, and the Mustang bucked to the side.

Towards me.

I froze. No time to move. No time to react.

Hands hit me from my left side, and I started to fall. The Mustang bore down on me. It clipped me on the hip. Pain exploded up and down my side. My feet left the ground, and I spun in the air.

Things got confusing. A yellow blur passing by me, almost through me. The screams from people on the street. My own screaming. The world spinning, too fast. Then nothing.

Some time passed, but not much. I opened my eyes. David Gomez stood above me, frowning in either confusion or concern or both. I felt grass beneath me, and a light spray of water coming from my right. With a groan, I sat up.

I was okay. My left side ached, but nothing felt broken. I could move. Pain radiated up and down one side of my body, but it was Tylenol pain, not Morphine pain.

The yellow car steamed and hissed a few feet away from me. An explosion of plastic and glass glittered on the sidewalk around me and the car. A cop, or maybe a guard from the courthouse, leaned into the Mustang and attended Ellis. From where I sat, half on the grass, half on the sidewalk, I could see Ellis slumped forward, a spiderweb of bloodied windshield in front of him.

Past the Mustang, more blood clung to the gray stone of the courthouse. Too much blood.

"James!" I pushed myself to my feet. Pain made me unstable. I started to fall, and David caught me.

"Easy," he said.

"The other guy. The one that was with me. Where is he?" I tried to go to the front of the car, but David held me back.

"He's gone, man. He saved you. Pushed you out of the way."

I pulled free of David's grip, limped past the open door of the mustang, ignored the words of the cop attending Ellis, and looked for myself. David was right. James hung over the crumpled hood, crushed between the car and the brick wall.

James had been right. Someone died that day, and I did blame myself.

• • •

Later, I sat in the office of The Society and told Pedro and Bobbie everything. It helped to get it all off my chest, but the guilt clung like tar. There would be no washing it away, not with words, nor with reassurances from my friends. However I looked at it, I traded one innocent man's life for another. Hell, if I hadn't gone snooping around the scene of the crime in the first place, no one would have died at all. David Gomez would have gone to jail, sure, but both he and James would still be alive.

Things went back to normal for a few days. I tried to get back to Society business, but they really didn't need me for a while. Everyone was off on different cases, and there weren't any hauntings for me to investigate. I wanted to distract myself with work, but the world had different ideas for me.

I learned my savior's full name. James Solomon Hatcher, to be buried after a small service three days after saving my life. He had never married, and he didn't have any family to speak of. Much later, I learned that Pedro had made the arrangements. In retrospect, he probably made sure I had time to grieve. There are always hauntings that need my attention, especially in Sacramento. Especially as we get closer and closer to The End Times.

The day of James' service, I showed up early. I dressed in my best jeans and my least torn Metallica t-shirt. I forgot to bring flowers. I was distracted, thinking maybe I shouldn't come at all, since I was the one responsible for him dying in the first place.

I stood at his fresh grave, wondering if I should say something and then leave. Cold ran down my right shoulder, as if I dumped my arm in a bucket of ice. I shivered and watched my breath form into mist. With a sigh, I opened my mind's eye and looked for the ghost.

James took a step back from me and crossed his arms in front of him. He wore the same clothes he wore the day he died, including his battered 49ers cap. "Hey, Mel."

"Oh no."

"What, you're not happy to see me?"

"I didn't mean-"

"It's okay." James raised a hand and moved as if to pat me on the shoulder, then stopped himself. He shook his head and laughed before taking a step back. "Well, hopefully I won't be here long enough that I have to get used to that. You got time to talk, buddy?"

"Whatever you need to help you move on, I'll do it."

"Whatever I need, huh?" A mischievous grin twisted his lips.

I held up my hands. "Before you get any ideas, just know that I'm not a medium."

"Noted. Actually, I think all I need is just a few minutes to talk to you."

I nodded. "Then let's talk."

James walked around me, his arms behind his back as he looked down at his grave. "Let's start with your questions, because I know you've got some."

"Why are you still here?" It was not what I meant to ask, but guilt forced the question out of my mouth.

"As I was dying, I knew that I set you up for the worst kind of guilt trip. I need you to understand that my death was not your fault."

"How is it not my fault? Everything that happened that day is because of decisions I made."

The air around me grew colder. James hit me with a hard stare. "Do you think the world revolves around you, boy? Are you standing at my grave, telling me that my decisions don't matter as much as your own?"

"No, I didn't mean-"

"I'm dead because I chose to save you. My decision. Not yours."

"But why?"

James sighed, and the cold of the ghost's emotions subsided. "Two reasons. The first is less important than the second."

"And that is?"

"I had cancer, Mel. I was going to be dead anyway. A year, maybe two at most."

I closed my physical eyes and lowered my head. It didn't matter. I could still see James through my mind's eye. But I didn't know what to say. News like that, you're supposed to give some kind of sympathy, but the usual social courtesies didn't really apply to this situation.

"The second reason," James continued, "is that you weren't going to let that boy go to prison for a crime he didn't commit."

I opened my physical eyes and frowned at James. "What does that have to do with anything?"

"I would have let him rot."

"I don't understand."

"I spent all of my years looking ahead, seeing what could happen, and making hard choices. I've had to choose the lesser of two evils so many times that letting someone like that Gomez kid go to prison wouldn't have even caused me to lose sleep."

"But you helped me save his life."

"Yeah, because if I didn't say anything, Gomez would have been run over on the street, and that psycho would have shot you a few weeks later while you tried to help Gomez's ghost."

I blinked. "You saw that?"

"I saw something like it. The future isn't set. But it's gonna get pretty bleak, and the world needs more people like you, that will stand up for something that is right. Instead of people like me."

He gave me too much credit, and I wanted to tell him so. But how could I? He sacrificed himself to save me. What kind of an asshole would I be to try and convince him that the one he sacrificed for wasn't worth it? Humility had its place, but not if it pushed James in the direction of becoming an angry spirit. "I believe you."

James closed his eyes and lowered his head. Ghosts don't need to breathe, but they still go through the motions, especially so close after the time of their death. James took a deep breath, let it out in a sigh, then opened his eyes, which were full of tears. "There's one last thing."

"What's that?"

"There's a plague coming. It won't be the end of the world, but it's coming. You and your friends need to be ready for it. The plague isn't the end of the world, but ask your friend Ortega about it. It's one of the signs of The End of Days."

I nodded slowly. I didn't need to ask about what James was talking about. I read some of the books myself. "I'll let Pedro know."

James smiled, and a single tear leaked from the corner of his eye and ran down his cheek. His aura shifted, and some of the darkness and lines of shadow that gave his spiritual form definition seemed to blur. "Okay, Mel. That's my cue. Thank you."

"What are you thanking *me* for? You saved my life."

James didn't answer. He smiled, turned sideways, and disappeared in golden light. With the light came an overwhelming sense of peace and warmth, which faded within minutes of James crossing over.

I've spent years helping ghosts find closure. It's a rare, precious thing when the ghosts help me find the same.

# AUTHOR'S NOTE

This is the continuation of the story of Mel Walker, a young scoundrel with a heart of gold and a psychic gift. The first book, *The Repossessed Ghost,* introduced Mel and his friends and set the stage for what is to come. Mel's world is our world, if our world contained ghosts and psychics and occasional magic users.

The events of *The Repossessed Ghost* took place in late 2012, and "The Psychic on the Jury" is set several years later. This story serves as a transition between the first novel and the second. And, being short, it offers a less expensive alternative for learning about Mel Walker and his adventures.

You can read this story first, no problem. But I think it's more fun to read *The Repossessed Ghost* first, if you dare.

# ABOUT THE AUTHOR

Hailing from sunny Sacramento, California, Brian C. E. Buhl is trying to save the world. Formerly enlisted in the U.S. Air Force, Brian now spends most of his time writing software for the solar industry. When he's not engineering technical solutions, he can sometimes be found playing saxophone with local community bands. Also, he writes science fiction and fantasy.

# ALSO BY THE AUTHOR

## THE REPOSSESSED GHOST
by Brian C. E. Buhl

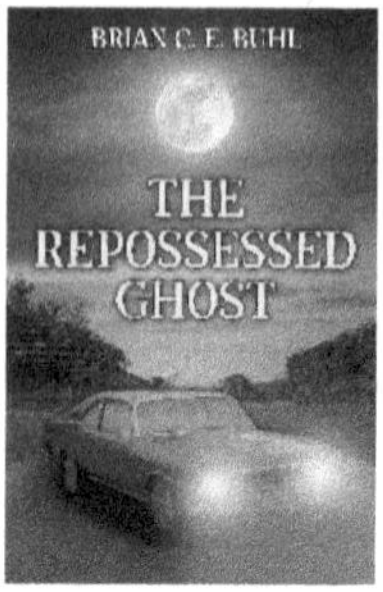


*Do you think ghosts haunt only houses?*

As a repo man, Mel just pulled off the smoothest take of his life. Kate, a college student, was undecided on which major to pursue. All of their plans went out the window the night Mel found Kate in the back of a '74 Nova.

## ONE FOR THE ROAD
by Melissa M. Buhl & Brian C. E. Buhl

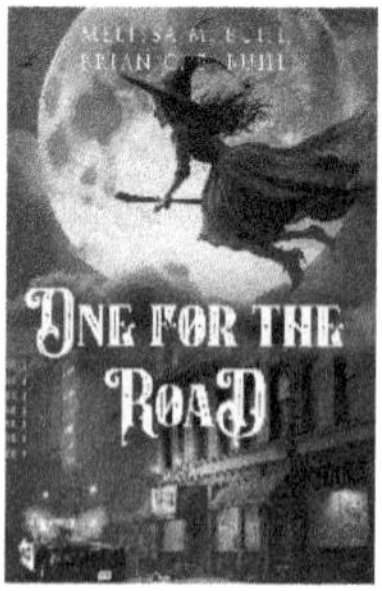


*Tina knows tracking spells, and her best friend Alexa knows how to get into trouble.*

When Father Time goes missing, it's up to both of them to use their wits and their magic to bring him in. If Father Time isn't there for the New Year's ritual, it will be certain doom for the entire city.

# YOU MIGHT ALSO ENJOY

## CHOOSE YOUR TRUTH

by Jo Miles

*Truth is obsolete. May the best lies win.*

## CONSIDER THE POSSIBILITIES

by Stephan James

*Waking to find a time-displaced army recruiter at your door?*

*Just a typical Saturday morning.*

## WE HAVE ALWAYS LIVED IN THE BREAK ROOM

by Michael Allen Rose

*Wahl'ter Dinsdale has been the master accountant for the tribe of the break-room for many seasons. But even he is not prepared when strange rumors reach the tribe of an unsettling phenomenon.*

Milton Keynes UK
Ingram Content Group UK Ltd.
UKHW010839130724
445228UK00015B/23

9 781962 538985